A JUST ONE MORE BOOK
Just For You

Where's That Duck?

by Mary Blocksma

Illustrated by Sandra Cox Kalthoff

Developed by The Hampton-Brown Company, Inc.

CHILDRENS PRESS ®

CHICAGO

Word List

Give children books they can read by themselves, and they'll always ask for JUST ONE MORE. This book is written with 78 of the most basic words in our language, all repeated in an appealing rhythm and rhyme.

a	for	me	see
alone	four	more	stuck
and	Fox('s)	must	
as	from		telephone
	fun	nearly	that('s)
back		not	the
be	get	now	them
but	go		then
	got	number	there('s)
can(not)		of	those
Chuck	having	on	three
come	hear	one	to
count	help	onto	town
	her	or	two
do		out	
down	I('ll)		was
duck(s)	in	passed	went
	is	put	what
everyone	it's		will
		quack	with
fat	just		
fence		ride	you
find	let('s)		
fooling	look	sack	
flew		said	
		saw	

Library of Congress Cataloging in Publication Data

Blocksma, Mary.
  Where's that duck?

  (A Just one more book just for you)
  Summary: Chuck the mule goes to town to retrieve four wandering ducks, who are unaware they are being stalked by a hungry fox.
  [1. Ducks—Fiction. 2. Mules—Fiction. 3. Stories in rhyme] I. Kalthoff, Sandra Cox., ill. II. Hampton-Brown Company. III. Title. IV. Series.
PZ8.3.B5983Wh 1985   [E]   85-15001
ISBN 0-516-01587-7   AACR2

Four ducks saw a fence,
and the fence was down.
"Quack!" said the ducks.
"Let's go to town!"

"Look!" said Chuck. "The fence is down.
Those ducks got out and went to town."

4

"I must get those fat ducks back,
or Fox will put them in that sack."

6

Duck Number One
was having fun
fooling nearly everyone.

"I hear a duck!" said Chuck.
"I do.
Come out now, Duck.
I'll count to two.

"ONE... TWO...!"

"There!" said Chuck. "Now I see you!
Let's go look for Duck Number Two."

"Chuck," said the duck, "that's what I'll do, but you must let me RIDE on you!"

Duck Number Two was not alone.
That duck was on the telephone!

"I hear a duck!" said Chuck. "I do.
Come out now, Duck! I'll count to two.

"ONE… TWO…!"

"Duck," said Chuck. "It's you I see.
Let's go find Duck Number Three."

"Chuck," said the duck, "that's what I'll do. But you must let me RIDE on you!"

Duck Number Three, as you can see,
was just as stuck as a duck can be.

"I hear a duck!" said Chuck. "I do.
Come out now, Duck! I'll count to two."

"ONE... TWO...!"

"Now," said Chuck, "there's just one more.
Let's go look for Duck Number Four."
Just then Fox passed them with that sack,
and the sack went…

"HELP!" said Chuck.
"GET that sack!"

"The duck is in there!
Get her back!"

Three ducks flew onto Fox's back.
One duck flew from Fox's sack.

Then Chuck and the ducks—
One, Two, Three, Four—
went back to the fence.
But there is MORE!

"There's JUST ONE MORE!"
said four fat ducks.
"There's one more duck
to look for, Chuck."

"But I can count four ducks,
I do!
There cannot be
one more of you."

"But I hear a duck!" said Chuck. "I do. Come out now, Duck. It's YOU!"